# BLUE CLAWS

# BLUE CLAWS

Written and illustrated by

## WALTER LYON KRUDOP

Atheneum 1993 New York

Maxwell Macmillan Canada
TORONTO
Maxwell Macmillan International
NEW YORK OXFORD SINGAPORE SYDNEY

Atheneum
Macmillan Publishing Company
866 Third Avenue
New York, NY 10022

Maxwell Macmillan Canada, Inc.
1200 Eglinton Avenue East
Suite 200
Don Mills, Ontario M3C 3N1

Macmillan Publishing Company is part of
the Maxwell Communication Group of Companies.

First edition

Printed in Hong Kong by South China Printing Company (1988) Ltd.

10   9   8   7   6   5   4   3   2   1

The text of this book is set in Baskerville.

The illustrations are rendered in oil paints.

Library of Congress Cataloging-in-Publication Data
Krudop, Walter, 1966-
Blue claws / written and illustrated by Walter Krudop.—1st ed.
p.    cm.
Summary: A young boy gets to know his grandfather better when the
two of them go crabbing in Long Island's Great South Bay.
ISBN 0-689-31787-5
[1. Grandfathers—Fiction.   2. Crabbing—Fiction.   3. Long Island
(N.Y.)—Fiction.]   I. Title.
PZ7.K938Gr   1993
[E]—dc20        92-9922

*For Sara*

"Bunker."

Grandpa whispered in his morning voice. "There's only one kind of bait to use for blue claws, and that's bunker. Today is a day for crabbing." I didn't understand, but I smiled and agreed. It was the first time I had ever stayed with Grandpa alone.

Grandpa pulled all kinds of gear to the back of the house. "This net's about had it. We'll double-knot this new one so we don't lose any of those blue claws." He ripped into the net with his pocketknife. When he was done he picked up the long net and the fat white bucket, and we started for the bait shop. It was a long way.

"I'm gonna need two nice-size bunker," Grandpa said to
the man in the white smock. Plop! The man smacked two
slimy fish onto stiff butcher paper and wrapped them up.

Small, skinny fish lay heaped together on packed ice.
"Those are shiners," the man told me. "Some people fry
them up, bones and all, and eat them."

I looked at the dead fish with their milky eyes staring past
me. "I'm not ever eating them!"

Outside, the sun crackled hot on the dock and Grandpa's heavy feet made the planks creak.

Grandpa fastened his line to the piling. I tried to do the same. "That's not how you do it," Grandpa snapped, and finished tying up my line. Sometimes Grandpa was hard to be with.

He unwrapped the fish. Tearing through the scales with his pocketknife, he cut the fish in half. "Here, tie this to your line," Grandpa said. I didn't want to touch the rotten-smelling fish, but I didn't want Grandpa to know. Holding my breath, I tied the slippery tail to the line. I hoped I tied it right.

We dropped our lines in the water and waited. There was nothing but bait on my line every time I pulled it up. The cord felt wet in my hands. Grandpa wasn't pulling on his line; he was very still. On my third try my line was a little harder to pull up, and as the bait came close to the surface, there was something attached to it.

"Grandpa! I caught one!"

I pulled the line up and Grandpa readied the net. "Got ya!" Grandpa said as he netted the angry crab and plopped it into the bucket. I felt good. I even saw Grandpa smile a little.

As I threw my line back in, Grandpa was pulling his up. Two giant blue claws were fighting over his bait. I held one crab down with the net. Grandpa went after the other one.

"Crabs are smart," Grandpa said, crouching over the one trying to escape. "Always pick 'em up from behind; that way they can't pinch you." Crabs must be smart, because he got pinched right on the thumb. I couldn't help but laugh.

We sunk our lines back in. I sat down on the dock and
hung my legs over the edge. I liked sitting on the dock and
not thinking about anything.

"Some of those crabs don't look big enough to keep. We're gonna have to throw some back," Grandpa said. I didn't mind; our bucket was getting full. I was sure we had enough for supper. So we wound up our lines and packed up our gear.

Two older men with crab cages appeared at the end of the dock. We offered them our bait since we were leaving. "Any luck?" they asked.

"We caught a few blue claws," I said as we passed them.

"We sure did," Grandpa agreed.

Our shoes were sloshy wet, so we hung them on the
clothesline along with Grandpa's big undershirts. My hands
smelled like fish no matter how many times I washed them,
and my hair was sticky with salt water.

After we cleaned up, Grandpa boiled some water in his

copper kettle. When the crabs hit the water, they turned a
brilliant red. The funny smell of cooked crabs floated into
every room in the house.

We ran the crabs under cold water. Crunch! One after the
other, we scooped the buttery meat out of the shells. The
claws tasted best.

I kept the biggest crab shell for myself. I decided to hang it on my wall when I got home, but for now I would just put it on Grandpa's bookshelf.

"Looks like bishop's rain," Grandpa said as he pointed out the back door. We watched the storm clouds surround the house. "See the way it falls," Grandpa said, "at a slant, the way a bishop moves in a chess game."

When the rain stopped, we sat on the front porch and watched the bulrushes sway with the waves. That night the bay was quiet except for the circle sounds the wind made around the tall boats.

I thought about the day and the rain and the crabs.

I saw Grandpa thinking, too.